SERIE d'ECRITURE
No. 15

Pascal Quignard

ON WOODEN TABLETS
APRONENIA AVITIA

Translated from the French by Bruce X

BURNING DECK, PROVIDENCE
2001

SERIE d'ECRITURE is an annual of current French writing in English translation. The first five issues were published by SPECTACULAR DISEASES, which continues to be the sole source for European distribution and subscription. Since No. 6, the publisher has been Burning Deck in Providence, RI.
Editor: Rosmarie Waldrop

Individual copies $10. Subscription for 2 issues: $16.
Supplements: $5.
In England: £5. 2 issues: £8. Postage 25p/copy.
Distributors:
Small Press Distribution, 1341 Seventh St,. Berkeley CA 94710
1-800/869-7553; orders@spdbooks.org
Spectacular Diseases, c/o Paul Green, 83b London Rd., Peterborough, Cambs. PE2 9BS
US subscriptions only: Burning Deck, 71 Elmgrove Ave., Providence RI 02906

Cet ouvrage, publié dans le cadre d'un programme d'aide à la publication, bénéficie du soutien du Ministère des Affaires Etrangères et du Service Culturel de l'Ambassade de France aux Etats-Unis.
This work, published as part of a program of aid for publication, received support from the French Ministry of Foreign Affairs and the Cultural Services of the French Embassy in the United States.

Burning Deck is the literature program of Anyart: Contemporary Arts Center, a tax-exempt non-profit corporation.

ISSN 0269-0179
ISBN 1-886224-45-5

Originally published as *Les tablettes de buis d'Apronenia Avitia* by Editions Gallimard, Paris, 1984. All rights reserved.

© 1984 by Editions Gallimard
Translation © 2001 by Bruce X

Cover by Keith Waldrop

CONTENTS

I. Life of Apronenia Avitia   7

II. On Wooden Tablets: Apronenia Avitia   27

    Chapter I (folio 482 recto to folio 484 verso)   29
    Chapter II (folio 485 recto to folio 490 recto)   37
    Chapter III (folio 490 verso to folio 495 recto)   47
    Chapter IV (folio 495 verso to folio 499 verso)   55
    Chapter V (folio 500 recto to folio 505 verso)   63
    Chapter VI (folio 506 recto to folio 512 recto)   73
    Chapter VII (folio 512 verso to folio 518 recto)   85
    Chapter VIII (folio 518 verso to folio 524 recto)   95

I
LIFE OF APRONENIA AVITIA

Apronenia Avitia was born in 343. Constantine ruled the empire. She was 70 years old when she died. Powerful and a patrician, she spent the greater part of the year in her Roman palaces or in her wealthy villa on Mount Janiculum. In letters and in a daybook kept in imitation of Paulinus and Rutilius Namatianus, not a single remark alludes to the end of the empire. Either because she was above seeing. Or because she didn't see. Or because modesty kept her from saying. Or in the conviction that seeing was irrelevant. This contempt and indifference earned her the contempt and indifference of historians. The death of Magnence, the execution of Gallus, the accession of Julian as head of the empire, Jovian, Valentinian, Valens: not a single of these names passed her lips. She saw Alaric in Rome, and her only concern was to note the grainy luminous thickness of a fog rising, fishermen floating down the distant Tiber. The Battle of Mursa, the Battle of Argentoratum, Battle of Marcianopolis and Battle of Andrinopolis, the successive incursions of Franks, Alamanni, and Saxons into Gaul, and likewise Goths and Alani into Pannonia, Bastarns and Huns along the Danube, Saxons invading Brittany, Vandals and Suevi in Spain — it was as if no sounds came forth from these clashing swords, as if victim blood gushing over stone pavements, rushing through burning straw fields, spurting over the marble of besieged or ruined palaces remained invisible. She was younger than Symmachus or Ambrose. Older than Augustine or Jerome. Through Decimus Avitius, she was related to Vettius Agorius Praetextatus and to Aconia Fabia Paulina, to Virius Nicomachus Flavianus, to Rusticiana, to Lycoris, to Lampadius, to the elder Melania, and to the Anicii. A second marriage only further complicated the network of friendship and genealogy that, in ways, was right from the beginning hopelessly tangled.

In 350 the Salian Franks settled Toxandria. Apronenia Avitia had as her nurse a young woman originally from the Setia region. She had the name Latronia and was born during the era of Constantine's Vicennalia. She died brutally three years later (year: Magnence's death) near the end of a banquet, raped and brutally dismembered at age 22, by friends of D. Avitius and, as speculation had it, by D. Avitius himself. In 357, with Memmius Vitrasius Orfitus as Roman prefect the second time and Sextus Claudius Petronius Probus the proconsul of Africa, Decimus Avitius gave away in marriage his eldest, Apronenia Avitia, to Appius Lanarius. The same year in Thagaste in Numidia, a small pockmarked bandylegged, spindly-armed African boy, hardly able to walk and answering to the name Augustine, would play in shadows of magically white alleys bathed in a thick light. He'd awkwardly hurl nuts at quail, at domestic nightingale. His father was Patricius. The age of his mother and that of Apronenia Avitia are approximately the same. She's Christian and she tipples. Her name is Monica.

•

In 360 as Sextus Aurelius Victor was finishing his *Caesars*, Apronenia Avitia had already given birth to two daughters, Flaviana and Vetustina. Through her father, the young patrician was related to the pagan party's most powerful families. In the two Roman palaces owned by Appius Lanarius, she welcomed Rusticiana and her eight year old boy, as well as Aconia Fabia

Paulina, Melania the Elder, and Anicia Proba. In company with A. Lanarius she was received at the home of Sex. Claudius Petronius Probus and into a pagan society favored by the emperor.

In 364 L. Aurelius Symmachus, the father of Symmacha, was Urban Prefect. In a suite of little rooms opening over the Sublicius bridge, she is introduced to a certain Q. Alcimius and begins a five year (365-370) relationship with him. In 369 Quintus Aurelius Symmachus returns the conquered Trier gold to the Prince. Afterward, she breaks off with Q. Alcimius. She gives us an account of the scene — a mid-day assignation at the Rostra, sharp insults, pain, Silig standing her up, a vision of the Gorgon lasting two or three hours — and finally, sobs. As the glory of her closest friends increases, she herself remains practically unknown. She luxuriates in obscurity and welcomes it. She combines a few pieces of straw, animal hair, mosses, leaves, and flowers — splendidly obscure nests, immense termitaria, constructed for her atop City hills. In 370 Memmius Vitrasius Orfitus gave his daughter Rusticiana to Q. Aurelius Symmachus and in 371 Sextus Claudius Petronius Probus is imperial coadjutor. By the year of Valentinian II's proclamation, Apronenia Avitia had given birth to seven children who survived their second year, all outliving her.

The first Apronenia Avitia letter, still extant, dates from 379, when Flavius Afranius Syagrius is African proconsul and Decimus Magnus Ausonius is consul. This is the year immediately preceding Theodosius's edict. Two kinds of work bearing Apronenia Avitia's name have come down to us, *epistolae* and *buxi*. The term *buxi* refers to certain wooden tablets, on which antiquity noted debts, credits, births, disasters, and deaths. Apronenia began keeping what might be styled notes, jottings, "strings tied around her finger," daily memoranda, starting the year of Theodosius's death, 395 AD. This year also marks the death of her father, D. Avitius, following Virius Nicomachus Flavianus's suicide. It is the year of Apronenia Avitia's second marriage to Sp. Possidius Barca. She's 51 or 52.

These notes break off the year Athaulf marries Galla Placidia — 414 AD. By now Apronenia Avitia is 71. We're probably right to assume the end of this journal coincides with her death.

The correspondence still extant under Apronenia Avitia's name begins with the year 379 but doesn't allow much greater precision. There are no extant letters after Stilicho's murder on August 22, 408 — and in any case, none after the orders to destroy the inscriptions in the Forum Romanum praising Stilicho's loyalty to the empire and celebrating his victories (*Quamvis litteras meas...*, folio 481recto).

There exists only a single edition of the letters and the wooden tablets. This appears in the Paris 1604 reissue of Father Juret's collection: *Quinti Aurelii Symmachi v.c. / Cons. ordinarii, et praefecti Urbi / Epistolarum Lib. X castigatissimi. / Cum auctuario. L. II. / Cum Miscellaneorum L. X. / Et Notis nunc primum editis / a Fr. Jur. D. / Parisiis, Ex Typographia Orriana. Anno Christiano 1604. Cum privilegio Regis.* This reissue has been augmented with manuscripts from Father Pithou's collection and thus represents a more generous selection of Low Latin texts than the preceding, which, dated 1580, has circulated rather widely. J. Lect reproduces only the text of the first edition. Apronenia Avitia's *Epistolae* appear in folios 342 through 481 of the Paris 1604 reissue. The three remaining letters from 380 have nothing to say about the state of the empire, about the progress of the Christian party, about the Theodosian edict, or about the destruction of the Victory altar. Apronenia Avitia lived to see the extremely rapid political advance of that party (that is, the Christian) though her work fails even to mention its name. The age was extraordinary, however. The sheer resonance of its proper names, little by little inscribed into canonical legend, already seems terrifying, thick, coagulated, deaf, and medieval, as if inseparable from the very texture of a not yet existing language: Didymus, Bonosus, Damasus, Siricius, Optatus, Sidonius, Martin, Hilary, Paulinus, Macrobius. And even an unknown would be called Ambrosiaster.

In 385 the letter of Apronenia Avitia specifies *"A. d. tertium nonas octobres primo lucis..."*: October 5, 385, at dawn. In his Aventine palace, a fit of apoplexy strikes Appius Lanarius, who never fully recovers. A. Lanarius is 73 years old, Apronenia Avitia 42. Not far off in Milan that same year, in early afternoon, municipal rhetor Augustine is greatly touched on hearing a child's song, in a garden set aside for his use. He hears the refrain on rising from under the shade of a chestnut tree, as he says, to move to a climbing fig's paler shade. This same year Saint Jerome suddenly abandons Rome for Jerusalem.

In 386 Flavianus Gorgonius is *comes rei privatae*. Appius Lanarius's illness appears hopeless, and Apronenia gives away Flaviana and Aufidia in marriage. By 387 all of her children have married. Symmachus is prince of the senate. In 389 when Nicasius is co-consul with Timasius, A. Lanarius, born the very year of the battle of Milvius, dies at age 77. Apronenia Avitia leaves us with little information on the subject of this first husband, with whom nevertheless she shares 32 years of married life (with seven surviving children). The 4 or 5 years directly following A. Lanarius's death seem for Apronenia Avitia to have been a period of some confusion. Shamelessly opportunistic, most of her friends appear to have joined the Christian party. Alypius, a Christian, is City prefect. Nicasius dies. And the pressures exerted by the Christians continue, or even increase. One of D. Avitius's closest friends, Virius Nicomachus Flavianus, backed into a corner through a combination of juridical blackmail and arbitrary seizure of his Campanian and Sicilian estates, is forced into suicide. The senate is afraid to do anything. On September 5, 394 Virius kills himself. Less than four months after his father's death, Nicomachus Flavianus the Younger converts, thus avoiding Christian reprisals. Whether Apronenia Avitia, mother-in-law of Nicomachus, herself considered that course of action remains unknown. The correspondence of this period —

Apronenia is a widow and not yet 50 — is contradictory and in certain ways confused. A series of four rather odd letters appears in the folios 401-416 of the Juret collection, Paris reissue. The letter *Facio rem cum tuis moribus* (folio 411 recto) can be summed up this way: in 392, having briefly mentioned Anicia Proba and the age-old friendship linking the two families, the patrician Apronenia Avitia, 49 year old widow of A. Lanarius, seeks pious counsel of the Roman ecclesiastical authorities, to plan her future. The priest, Nasebus, advises her to resist the affectionate pressures from her father urging her to remarry, counsels a vow of celibacy to God, advises applying prayer in repentance for her past impurities. Nasebus's letter to Apronenia Avitia has been preserved in toto (*Auctus sum gaudio....*, folio 412, verso). Here is its peroration: "Do your best to restore an innocence that age and pleasure have besmirched and a purity that time, maternity and sensuality have sullied. At least strive to rekindle in yourself the yearnings for that state. Pledge yourself to avoid the perils of exposure to Rome, food, a taste for profane books, concern for your body, for wealth, for your advancing age and the self-centeredness linked to it, for music and for all the arts. Purify yourself! Realize the filthiness of the matrimonial state! Be moved by Our Lord's state, by the virtue of poverty, by contempt for this world, by detachment from human society, and by a love for heaven." We don't know what exactly occurred in the meeting with Nasebus. Apronenia Avitia doesn't appear to have been absolutely convinced. She doesn't turn her back on the Whore of Babylon. She doesn't join nuns living in Palestine. In 395 at the age of 51 or 52 she marries a second time. Her husband is Sp. Possidius Barca, the great landowner and senator. As far as we can tell she loves her husband. In a rather crude letter (*Meae litterae quoniam tibi....*, folio 435, verso) dated March 399 and addressed to Eudoxia, she describes sex with him as primitive and overeager, but, she adds, with something sweet and nearly playful to it.

•

In 394, deeply affected by the suicide of Virius Nicomachus Flavianus, Decimus Avitius dies. Apronenia Avitia supplements income from his considerable properties with her widow's pension. She combines this in 395 with the patrimony of her new husband. Finally, using a stylus, she begins jotting the odd little notes on wooden tablets. Her precise motives for the descision to write the *buxi* — the marriage with Sp. Possidius, the death of D. Avitius — remain unknown. But if the name *buxi*, traditionally retained as title for Apronenia Avitia's work, is not unquestionably of her own making, the name isn't wholly arbitrary either: in fragment CLIII Apronenia Avitia speaks of tablets (*tabellae*) and fragment CXX alludes to the fragrance of the wooden tables (*buxi*) being written upon. Considering the era, Apronenia Avitia's *Wooden Tablets* is a relatively uncommon work. In general, few examples have come down to us of this type of daybook composed by antiquity's landowners and wealthy aristocrats. More than that, considering the time of its appearance, the work is doubly odd. A 69 year old woman itemizes accounts, errands to be done, investment returns, as well as purchases of cloth, antique statues, orders for wine and pefume, rare art-works, even preferences for and aversions to — odors and pleasures, paradoxes, jokes, nasty gossip, vulgarities, nightmares, memories. Powerfully concrete, hypochondriac, Roman — and if nothing is known of her reading and upbringing, everything is known of her preferences and physical habits, the sounds she feared for power to stir old memories, the food and wine she valued above anything. This diary exemplifies writers who suddenly, unexpectedly respond to commands imposed no doubt by awareness of death, but steeped in a hypochondria requiring an immediate and scrupulous itemization of health states, particularities about meals, crises, moods, bouts with insomnia. Ailios Aristeides in second century Symrna, Sei Shonagon in 11th century Kyoto, Pontormo in 16th century Florence, and Samuel Pepys in 17th century London — all probably responded to similar needs.

All of a sudden, just listing complaints seems a way to contain if not surmount them. You think by setting ailments down in writing you can control a body that emptiness keeps chipping away — shoring it up with a scaffolding of isolation and cementing it. You attempt to contain water leaking through the fingers, however tight your grip. What could be more foolish? In contrast to Vivia Perpetua of the prior century, it's unlikely Apronenia Avitia considered publishing — communicating to a public — what she'd hastily noted. Still, in 459 at the age of 83 Paulinus de Pella published his *ephemerides*. The Latin text of the *Buxi* appears in folios 484 through 524 of Father Juret's compendium. I was struck by the oddity of the *Buxi* texts. It seemed to me if readers agreed to lend warmth and breath, these odors, dreams, garments, and forms would revive and take on movement — this ancient ghostliness, this phantom of a woman would also resurrect the memory of a body once alive.

•

In 396, nothing. An empire splits. Seated with the Curia, Spurius Possidius Barca is present for the famous entrance of widower Pammachius taking his place among colleagues at senate meetings dressed in monk's clothing. He must have been part of the silence, the incomprehension greeting him. In her letter *Quotiens tua sumo conloquia...*, Apronenia Avitia forcefully portrays the mute shock, astonishment, and stupor into which the assembled senators were at first sunk, the murmurings, the gradual recovery from lethargy, the sudden mounting of a wave of voices, the despair and sincere anguish felt by the assembled senators, confronted with the dark provocative garment, among purple-bordered white linen togas betokening senatorial dignity. Senator P. Saufeius Minor rises and silence ensues. Without raising his voice though perhaps marking his words with a certain emphasis, he says that this garment within the Curia walls is worse than the Huns at the frontier.

In the years that followed, and up to the death of Publius and beyond the sadness of her second widowhood, the friendship between this woman and this man put forth twigs and branches, growing odd new leaves, comprising what might be called entire forests of idle conversation between two old people; a rhapsody of remembered stale wit; grievance and grief as implacable as death's approach — what might be called a singular and morbid competition.

In 397 Aurelius Ambrosius dies at Milan. It was said of him that death intervened as he wrote the word *mortem*. In 399 Nicomachus Flavianus Junior is the City prefect. (More than 30 years later, in 431, the Christian party forces the father of this Nicomachus, Apronenia's son-in-law, to commit suicide. He himself joins that party, becoming pretorian prefect of Italy, of Illyricum and of Africa. Sitting in his personal library comprising three halls and a hydraulic organ, he revises the complete works of Titus Livius.)

In 401 Andromachus is prefect of the Gauls. The same year sees Quintus Fabius Memmius Symmachus, son of Symmachus and Rusticiana, marry. In a letter dated December, 401 (*Mones ut amicitiae...*, folio 444, recto) Apronenia Avitia records a sortie in company of Aufidia and Fabricius, to the Porta Portuensis, to check on construction work. It's with the help of this notation, moreover, that the letter is dated. Still, not a word to help explain the restoration of the Aurelian Wall. Nothing about Stilicho or the advance of Alaric's Goths or the panic assumed by historians to be raging in Rome. Nothing about famine, the rationing of bread at two-thirds rate, the interruptions of traffic on the Tiber, or the first cases of cannibalism. Merely an allusion (*Nihil moror ceteros...*, folio 445, recto) to the stench throughout the city. (The Gothic troups having occupied the gates, the Roman dead aren't removed for burial in the suburban cemeteries.)

In contrast, it seems to me, the letter *Facit enim tenerior...* (folio 476, verso) should be dated from this first siege of Rome.

Apronenia Avitia asserts that she dedicated a small Teucter slave to the national gods, a boy who for months had been afflicted with fever and a terrible catarrh. Thus Apronenia Avitia takes sides in the debate raging among the besieged Romans and further separates herself from the Anicia Proba group. Refugees from Tuscany reported that, after ancient ritual sacrifices, the city of Narni was protected from these invasions. If the seizure of the empire by the Christian party was the source of the harm fallen on it, then a return to the national, proscribed gods would constitute the only protection from the invaders. Volusianus — to whom Apronenia Avitia is related through Melania the Elder — powerfully develops these arguments: the ancient gods are punishing Rome in its fall. The Roman Prefect fails to obtain from Pope Innocent I the dispensation for which he pleads. The pope consents to a celebration of national sacrifices providing they remain strictly familial and private, specifying that only the Christian sacrifices and manducation of the tortured god can take place publicly. The pagan party objects. The ancient sacrifices will lose all power to protect the imperial capital if not offered publicly to the national gods in accord with time-honored custom, and in the presence of the senatorial body. The senate doesn't dare offend the Christian party. A contribution of wealth is voted. Promised to the Goths — five thousand pounds of gold, thirty thousand of silver, the freeing of all Gothic and foreign slaves, four thousand silken tunics, three thousand purple-died skins, three thousand pounds of spice. The Christians rise up. The sequestering, for state benefit, of the landed estates held by Pinianus and Melania of the Christian party, the wealthy owners of the Valerii palace, is described as "a theft from Christ" (the bloody idol of the Christians). The Christians stone the prefect Pompeianus as he begins to sequester the Christian millionaires' properties. The senate has no choice but to turn on the pagan party. It gives orders to despoil all temples except those of the Christians. It votes a melting of gold and silver statues of Roman and foreign gods, exempting the god of the Christians. Romans who are still faithful to the traditional religion sadly wander through a Rome whose immense, tutelary, and glorious likenesses of the gods have been melted down. Zosimus reports that, as the goddess Virtus was carted off in her chariot to the foundry, a Roman citizen named Saufeius chancing on the scene raised his arms in lamentation, saying "Rome is losing its virtue." This Saufeius of Zosimus is, as it seems, the same as the senator P. Saufeius Minor who is the subject of so much discussion in the *Buxi*. Sozomenus (*Hist. eccles.*, IX, 6) — of the Christian party himself — mocks the pagans for sacrificing to gods who vanish in a day. In the same passage he pokes fun at their persistent and ill-fated stubbornness, pointing out that even the Gothic troops besieging them are turning to Christianity. It's against this background, it seems to me, that we have to read the letter *Facit enim tenerior...*: here again, Apronenia distances herself (though this time a little further) from the Anicia Proba group. And her "dedicating" her slave to Roman gods is probably sacrifice (disguised cannibalism?). But nothing indicates if the letter dates from the first siege, the siege of 409 (when Anicia Proba and the entire Anicii clan oppose Attalus even though he allows the Gothic bishop Sigesar to baptize him a Christian), or from Alaric's third siege of August, 410. It's during the course of the latter that cases of cannibalism are most numerous, though the witnesses' reports may exaggerate: Christians devouring pagans, mothers devouring "quite young children" as Saint Jerome writes (*Epist. ad Principiam*, CXXVII, 12). Augustine immediately rejoins — "this is nothing! During the siege of Samaria under King Benabad there was trafficking in edible infants, and the price of dove turds tripled." But the occasion for the most vigorous debate on ancient sacrifice is the time of the first siege. (The gods lost much of their appeal upon being melted). So I incline to the siege of 408.

Apronenia is 61 years of age as, on a winter day, January 15, 404, she instructs servants to bring up a small fire-pan and some Massic wine to the second *exedra* of her villa on Mount Janiculum, as, holding the lyre, she accompanies Olus, Flaviana and Lycoris, singing the Salii songs and the hymn to Tuchulcha.

Far away in Palastine, eleven days later, on January 26, in a cold cell on a rush mat, Jerome kneels near the sweating, hiccuping body of Saint Paula, assisting her in her death struggle — which he boldly refers to as a "psalm" — as her daughter Eustochium raises her arms into the darkened air and pours oil into the lamp attached to the wall.

•

In 404, the poet Claudius Claudianus dies. Throughout the year 404, Sp. Possidius's infirmities, nauseas, catarrhs, and fainting fits grow worse. Spurius Possidius Barca dies as the year 405 begins. The *Buxi* speak at length and in some detail of Possidius's sickness and death. Combined with inheritances from A. Lanarius, D. Avitius, and Sp. Possidius, Apronenia Avitia's wealth appears, at the end of her life, to have been considerable. All the same there's likelihood that Apronenia Avitia met with certain difficulties, owning no doubt to the terrible upheavals then shaking the empire and leaving it in the hands of the religiously inclined. At least with the death of Sp. Possidius Barca, but beginning in the year 404, the sudden frequency of allusions to accruing calendar interest and to receipt of bags of gold allows the supposition that Apronenia Avitia is experiencing difficulties in her affairs. With the help of the correspondence, a list can be drawn up: at least three palaces in Rome, two *villae* in the Roman suburbs, one of them on the Appian way, two rural *villae*, a villa in Naples, several *praedia* in Samnium, Apulia, Mauretania, property on the isle of Megaris, and the Sicilian palace bought back from Anicia Proba. A large portion of properties of the children of the first marriage have to be noted too. Though it actually appears to have been solely the villa-palace on the Janiculum — a property inherited from her father but coming through her mother and passed on as a dowry at the time of the second marriage in 395 — that the elderly patrician lady seems to have chosen as residence, at least during the very last years of life. The number of Sp. Possidius Barca's slaves, tenant farmers, and clients is estimated at between six and seven thousand. When Apronenia Avitia leaves one of her Roman palaces to go to the not too distant villa on Mount Janiculum, she notes that 110 persons follow her with 40 chariots. P. Saufeius speaks of an "entire village" working in the kitchens of his aging friend.

In 408 Nicomachus Flavianus becomes City prefect a second time. In spring Lampadius finally secures an agreement from the senate not to approve the four thousand pounds of gold Stilicho promised Alaric. At the beginning of winter, the Honorian Edict, dated November 15, 408, abruptly decrees the desctruction of all statues not the object of Christian worship: they're pulled off their pedestals, their inscriptions blotted out, their altars destroyed. As the Roman nobility watches, mallets are raised and workmen move on the divine simulacra to take them off to the foundry: the Roman gods, they realize, have definitively abandoned the world they till now protected. Conversions are rampant among Roman gentry. In 408 Apronenia watches as Melania the Elder's granddaughter Melania the Younger, who much earlier had gone over to the Christian party, leaves Rome accompanied by her husband Pinianus, her mother, Rufinus the learned exegete, and consecrated virgins recruited from among her slaves. Melania departs from Rome to take refuge in vast and luxurious estates she owns near Messina on the Sicilian coast, as Rufinus commences his Origen translations among marble statues in yew and boxwood gardens and a little walled-in date grove.

Volusianus — the uncle of Melania the Younger and Pinianus — remains in Rome and, still faithful to traditional religion, draws closer to the P. Saufeius Minor group as it meets on the Caelius hill. To his niece he writes vehement and, in many ways, remarkable letters: and then, like a child seized with a sudden impulse to communicate, didactic and proselytizing, he scatters his letters across the whole empire. Since Christianity has triumphed, life is less cheerful, he says. Because cities, streets, temples, theaters, and *thermae* haven't been maintained, they are deteriorating — gradually falling to pieces. Before the rise to power of the Christians, books were better written, life was slower and happier, prices not so high, women more beautiful, more radiant, more desirable, dwellings larger and more splendid, joy more contagious, light more dazzling, sounds purer, sex-smells more exciting and funkier; even the sardines and grilled sausages had another taste. Since the promulgation of Honorius's Edict, the loss of Rome's gods, and the presence of the Goths, Rome is devastated; wine has turned to blood, bread to fire and cinders; instead of songs and pantomime, there are only cries of the tortured; art has disappeared, there are only ruins. When ancient Romans sacrified to the ancient gods, Rome was a power to reckon with, it ruled the universe. Can the god of the Christians be much of a god if he hasn't protected his followers? Couldn't fifty just men have been found in Rome? And Rome is gone! Nowhere has the intercession of martyrs proved to be effective. The body of the Christian, Peter, didn't defend Rome. The body of the Christian, Paul, didn't defend Rome. The body of the Christian, Lawrence, didn't defend Rome. Volusianus tirelessly multiplies these arguments. Marcellinus condenses, summarizes, then sends them to Hippo, to Augustine, to Pinianus: to have them review them, respond. The first three books of *De Civitate Dei* scrupulously address the arguments of Volusianus and the party of the Roman *gens*: Alaric had respected the basilicas; there were fewer just men in Rome than in Sodom; the end of Rome was nothing compared to Gehenna and to Job's misery; the violated virgins should be envied because they acquired humility and Providence has demonstrated that purity isn't a physical good; God was right to punish the theaters.

In 409 Priscus Attalus, the administrator of the City as Curia legate, is proclaimed emperor by Alaric. The pagan party, reduced daily, becomes less and less relvant. Still, Priscus Attalus names Lampadius as pretorian prefect. Ambrosius Aurelius Theodorius Macrobius is proconsul of Carthage. Apronenia feels less drawn to the group around P. Saufeius Minor and their meetings on the Caelian hill palace than to the man himself, complicated, somewhat sentimental, paradoxical, nihilistic, and lonely. Moreover, the old patrician skeptic's influence on the senate seems to have fluctuated. Atala was deposed. Aurelius Prudentius Clemens dies writing the word *dolorosus*. On the night of August 24, 410, Apronenia Avitia's old friend Anicia Proba, who years before this had joined the Christian party, allows Alaric and his Gothic troups into Rome, by stealth, through the Porta Salaria. Anicia Proba (Procopius, *Bell. Vand.* I, 2) declares herself prompted by "charity in Christ, moved by the sufferings of the starving." The partisans of Priscus Attalus propose that Alaric and Proba are in love. The pagan party spreads around an admittedly rhetorical and somewhat dubious epigram, according to which, under a slave-god who has been the object of a dishonorable execution, we now are required to watch a Gothic pelt mating with a patrician toga. In part the words are libellous. As a letter from Jerome (*Epist. ad Demetriadem*, CXXX, 5) demonstrates, on the same night Anicia Proba gave orders to allow Alaric into Rome, Gothic soldiers were surrounding the Anicii palace, and Demetrias, the granddaughter of Anicia Proba, owed her escape from rape to the knife of her Batavian servant.

These scenes of pillage, arson, and massacre are renowned. Not a single word on the *villae* and palaces of Apronenia Avitia, of Lampadius, Fabius Symmachus, Nicomachus Flavianus or Publius Saufeius. Directly thereafter, Augustine (*Civ. Dei*, I, 1) makes fun of conservative Roman pagan citizens who, fearing massacre, rush for shelter to the churches. In my imagination I see Proba opening the Salarian gate to Alaric as simultaneously Apronenia and Saufeius kneel in a Christian basilica, pale, arms wrapped about each other. More easily I see Apronenia and her group, her family, her clients, and her slaves, in the course of that three day sack hiding in a corner of some palace, in some very ancient vaulted cellar going back to Augustus's day or Tiberius's, side by side, with the pale light of an oil lamp falling on them as they moan.

Anicia Proba, the younger Demetrias, and her mother leave Rome almost immediately on board a galley to join Jerome. The latter forbids Demetrias from marrying a refugee she's fallen in love with during the trip to Palestine: successfully convincing her to dedicate the rape she escaped to the god succoring her, in the form of perpetual virginity. Having removed her femininity from "Gothic impatience" she ought now to remove her ears from the "Fescennine songs" (Jerome, *Epist. ad Demetriadem*, CXXX, 7). On the other hand Jerome has nothing to say about the welcome accorded by the African Christian communities to those fleeing a burning city whose gates they themselves had opened to the arsonist, sheerly from religious conviction.

Anicia Proba succeeds, to an extent, in reconstituting a circle. She publicly expresses outrage at the way Heraclian, Count of Africa, pressed the refugees, fleeced them, then violated them. She asserts that Sabinus, Heraclian's son-in-law, sold the Syrian traders young Roman women already promised in marriage. At Anicia Proba's command a villa is built on what she refers to as the "holy places" — the Judean city of Jerusalem — which is to say the "true Rome, not the proud Babylon whose smoke still rises on Italian soil." Melania the Younger and Pinianus are present for the death of Tyrannius Rufinus at the estate of Messina and then leave for the monastery of Thagaste, joining Augustine at Hippo. At Hippo Pinianus decides to be a priest. Pinianus and Melania try to sell off their Italian and Sicilian holdings. Apronenia Avitia's Fragment LXI is the only passage alluding to the sudden influx of refugees on the coast of Africa, to the founding of a number of Palestinian colonies, and to their veritable proliferation following the sack of 410.

In 411 Apronenia witnessed the sale, by her old friend Melania the Elder's granddaughter, of the Valerii palace, half ruined, sacked by Gothic troops in the pillagings of August of the previous year. The entire Aventine is burned and deserted. The outer walls of the Decius *thermae* threaten to collapse. A decision is made not to rebuild the ruins of the temple to "Juno the Queen," and Christians pillage its marbles in broad daylight, to construct the church of St. Sabina. More and more, Apronenia is alone. Bleary-eyed and teetering, chafing, stuck in her Roman palaces (or what's left of them). A gray and red black-crested hoopoe, hidden in a huge dead tree-hole, nibbling on mossy dusty bark.

In December 412, her friend Publius Saufeius expires, surrounded by clients loyal to the party of the Roman gentry, in his luxurious, hieratic palace on Mount Caelius. He's a bit younger than Apronenia Avitia. Fragment CXXI of the *Buxi* suggests he loved her. In any case the account is Apronenia's — and the witness reduces the testimony almost to a dream.

In 414 Athaulf falls madly in love with Emperor Honorius's sister Galla Placidia. On January 1, 414 Athaulf and Galla Placidia are married at Narbonne, with Priscus Attalus intoning the epithalamium. Apronenia Avitia dies that spring. At least: the *Buxi* break off in spring 414. When she dies, Symmacus is dead, Stilicho is dead, Alaric is dead, Augustine and Jerome have long since stopped writing in their own hand; they sit on their thrones, their backs becoming straight and straighter; they tirelessly dictate to a small Teucter or Vandal *librarius* who sits at their feet.

II
ON WOODEN TABLETS
APRONENIA AVITIA

CHAPTER ONE

(folio 482 recto to folio 484 verso of the Parisian reissue of the Father Juret collection, Orrian, 1604)

I. Things to Do A. D. VI Kalendas

I'm going to the Numa temple.
Curtains of the litter.

II. Things that are Rare

Among things that are rare, I'll add books properly edited.
A man who ignores other men's looks.
Tweezers that really tweeze.
Windows that open, without letting light in.

III. Walking on the Island

On the Tiber I saw flat-bottom skiffs go by, laden down with oats, amphoras, wheat, fruit. Light skimmed over the water. The colors were truly lovely, especially the greens and blues. On the river banks — small naked children, splashing away, silently. They are too far away to hear and a wind was coming up out of the east. Nearby, at the edge of a tidal pool in the sedge, squatting, pink ass on his heels, a dark sun-burned five-year old boy is fishing for frogs. With a stern look, grabbing at his crotch, he shooes us away.

IV. Things to Do

To the Temple of Peace — before the spoils of Titus.
The phiala attributed to Mys.
The Via Tiburtina.
Wine from the hillside around Setia.

V. Lycoris Gives Birth to a Child

Lycoris gave birth to a child, who died not many hours later. I helped deliver it along with Spatale and Nigrina. The delivery rooms where the baby died repulse me. Lycoris had her servants bring in Syrian wine. This didn't do much for us. I felt miserable and it lasted till lunch, when I dined on oysters and boletus mushrooms.

VI. Something to Remember

The roundtable made of citron wood when we visited Glaucos.

VII. Different Kinds of Women

I despise women who think everything's wonderful, fabulous, fantastic.

I despise women who think everything's shallow, banal, stupid, pointless, or vulgar.

VIII. Things to Do

To the Colossus of Domitian on horseback.
A flowing cape fastened beneath the neck.
A holm-oak grove.
Peach trees grafted on apricots.
A mule costing as much as a young slave.

IX. Q. Alcimius

There was a time Quintus loved me. We were young. D. Avitius was still alive. He'd steal in by the second gate, with a whole night ahead! At dawn, he'd demonstrate such an unwillingness to get up, to leave me. He'd look around for his tunic — say how much leaving hurt him. He was in no hurry to lace his sandal-laces. He'd move over and kiss my face and under my belly. I'd wake up. Telling him anxiously, it's getting light outside, shouldn't you hurry? He'd sigh, and for me his sigh was like an echo of the river crossing Erebus. He'd sit on the bed without moving. He'd tie the sandal lacings. Then lean over whispering obscenities, or go on with some story he'd started in on, last night. He'd pour a little libation to honor the dawn. He'd wash his mouth with water and his crotch, rubbing his eyes. I'd slip up from behind. For a moment we'd stay there, before the double-paneled door, looking at each other. He'd say he hated spending the whole day apart from me. He said how the separation made him suffer. Four or five times, we'd repeat the rendezvous planned. My hand was on his arm. I touched his lips with mine. He'd cross the threshhold, then vanish. In the shadows I'd return to bed and stay sitting. Grateful for the night's events, I'd envy myself! I'd prop elbows upon thighs, inhaling the moistness, smelling my own sweetness, letting my hair down behind me. I'd be happy. But with the roosters crowing outside and the pails clattering — how to keep back the tears? I loved the distraction, stress, fatigue, confusion of smells, and bewilderment hard to tell from nauseated repletion, but which is brought on by excessive satisfaction.

X. Nurses

Antulla dismisses her nurse because her milk dried up.
Lycoris dismisses her Suevian nurse because she no longer has a child.

XI. Plecusa's Epigram about Sp. Possidius Barca

Lycoris says that 40 winters ago Spurius was quite handsome. Plecusa makes up this epigram:
"He still has those fine ears and there's still that unmistakable look."

XII. Things to Do A. D. VIII Idus

Off to Argiletum.

XIII. Spatale's Mirror

I asked Spatale to fetch a mirror. I looked at myself for a time. I spoke aloud these words.

"You're a monument from the days of Tarquin the Elder, unearthed by a farmer in the corner of some wheatfield."

I went off to eat sweetened suckling pig on a bed of cooked raisins. I drank two *setiers* of Massic.

XIV. Things that Cause Shame

Entering my husband's bedroom in the western wing of the palace and seeing him naked on all fours on top of the bed, with little valets around him, waxing him, and rubbing cold water on him, slapping salves onto him, helping him on with undergarments. It's mid-summer, the fire-pan ablaze. A little masseur removes hair from his ass and groin, except the scrotum.

CHAPTER TWO

(folio 485 recto to folio 490 recto)

XV. Young Men Leaning on Columns

Young men for the first time feeling the delights of languor.

Young men for the first time in their bodies feeling life-force ebb slowly into the western ocean each day, leaving behind fields of mussels and sandy beaches.

Young men morbidly considering an impulse to do themselves in, because of something just read in Greek, a teacher's sneer, the face of a Saburian girl. Shoulders against columns, standing there. The vague smell of milk and semen still on them. Their vacant eyes staring. Hair tumbling from the neck, wind from the *compluvium* sometimes parting it. Their skins shivering.

XVI. Cats and Partridges

I have two cats with little cuffs and yellow collars, partridges, and a blue ribbon — blue as Egyptian enamels.

XVII. The Little Dog

Muola, the little bitch born beneath Publius's bed, sleeps day and night, sleeps on her back. She breathes more gently than a child with milk still on its lips. At night I feel her paw pressing on the skin of my arm. She needs to piss.

XVIII. Something to Remember

The painted wood shows the *Parcae*'s distaffs.

XIX. Q. Alcimius

In response to the boldest, most timid of requests, because I loved the pleasures his limbs and voice steep me in, I stopped him from finishing his request. Without hesitation I said — yes.

XX. Nights of Famine

And nights we hadn't gasped at least three times, these were famine to us.

XXI. Things Giving the Feeling of Peace

I love the sound of carriages in Rome.
Hot baths on terrace gardens: at dusk.

The heavy sleep of a man who's just spurted.
Mattresses from the Nile.
Stars — and dawn blotting them out one by one.
I loathe old people. At least, the ones apparently never going anywhere without death as a companion.

XXII. Things to Do

Avenue of the Patricians.
Visting the Saepta.
The Murrhine marbled vase.

XXIII. Things to Do

Clay cups moulded from Sagonte earth.

XXIV. Things to Do

A sacrificial offering, a crow.
The twenty throw-cushions.
Eight two-wheel-carriage curtains.

XXV. A Smell I Hate

I hate the smell exuded by purple.

XXVI. *Sp. Possidius Barca's Palace on the Janiculum*

On an old property I have on the Janiculum, the one coming down as dowry from my mother, Spurius built a little villa. Southward, a vast parkland emerges from the ranging elevated table-lands — overlooking the hills, acting as barriers to the morning fogs. From the portico you can see Rome, make out the Alban hills, Tusculum slopes, ancient Fidenae, Rubrae, Anna Perenna's sacred groves. By their shapes and colors you can clearly pick out merchants and chariots, moving along Via Flaminia and Via Salaria. But sounds never reach us, not even iron wheels squeaking, porters' voices, boatmen's songs. The barges floating down the Tiber are distinctly visible. People and shapes appear as silent and distant as the stars just hours later, when you raise your head.

XXVII. *Smells I Hate*

Six smells I hate: the rank stinking of dried-up swamps.
A very small child spitting up mother's milk, on a tunic.
Vipers' nests.
A he-goat mounting a she-goat.
The bodies of very old men or very old women, even when bathed seven times.
Fleece twice plunged into a murex bath.

XXVIII. *Smells I Hate*

He takes my head between his hands. His hands stink of Trastevere.

XXIX. Smells I Hate

Smell of sulfur springs.
Pomade made from the dregs of Sabine wine.

XXX. The Drunken Spech of Sp. Possidius Barca

Spurius* got drunk and blubbery, he wouldn't stop going on about Gabba, his love of 40 winters earlier. Aconia Fabia Paulina and I hadn't yet become friends. This was the year Vettius Agorius Praetextatus was City prefect, and Flavius Afranius Syagrius was consul. When a man praises a woman he once loved, a person dead now — it's rather disagreeable. You're jealous of a body swallowed up by earth. And even the thought has been swallowed down into nothingness. You're stupid and unfair, even in your own eyes.

XXXI. Bags of Gold, Reeds

24 bags of gold.
247 quadrants.
Reeds from the Tagus for writing.

---

* "Barca" alludes to Hamilcar Barca, the cognomen of Spurius Possidius. The cognomen surely is derisory. Spurius Possidius stuttered, and it's quite likely that his being referred to as "Lightning" by senatorial colleagues was a jibe at this elocutionary shortcoming. Two epigrams have been preserved for us from a speech given before the Curia, and epigrams dedicated to the memory of the accomplishments of the prefect Memmius Vitrasius Orfitus.

XXXII. Discovery

Love-making during the first siesta doesn't appeal to me.

XXXIII. Conversation: Men's Desire

On the nostrils of Tronco, Spatale's dog, is a drop of mucous.
"You know, men have something like that, making them itch — at the tips of their *mentulas*," says Lycoris laughing.
"They call it desire, I think," says Marcella dryly.
"That's a strange way of putting it," says Plecusa gravely.
"The most universal things are seldom the most convincing," says Saufeius solemnly.
"For instance, death," says Lycoris slowly.
"For instance, the Roman language," says Spurius haltingly.
"For instance, the navel," says C. Bassus," or at least what that remnant suggests about us."
"For instance, all men including the Emperor in Milan," says Plecusa boldly.
"For instance, the pairing of our ears," says Marcella.
"I make an exception of how we absorb our food," says Lycoris. And to this contribution I nod approbation.
M. Pollio says the following: "Snails, thirsty for humidity* and needing the liquid that drops from heaven, don't go to the forum and crawl secretly into the cunts of consular wives but attempt to live off their own substance."

---

*The Latin text goes "...cum sitiunt umoris atque illis de caelo nihil liquitur."

XXXIV. More about Men's Desire

Plecusa is covered in makeup.
"The face you show doesn't sleep with you," says Caius.
"The face men hide sleeps at the base of their bellies," rejoins Plecusa.

XXXV. Things to Do

Mule.
Wolf.
Spotted Numidian chickens.
Colchidian pheasants.

XXXVI. Things to Do

Mallows against constipation.
Lettuce.

XXXVII. Theological Controversy

"The gods abandonned us starting with Julian," says C. Bassus.
"God abandonned us starting with Augustus," says M. Pollio.
"The gods abandonned us starting with Numa," says Ti. Sossibianus.
"The gods abandonned us starting with before whatever ever was," says P. Saufeius.

XXXVIII. Memories of Q. Alcimius

I used to love Quintus's light snoring. He would heave a sigh and then turn over in sleep.

XXXIX. Scary Sounds

As I child I was afraid of the sound of bronze — as hammered out on smoking anvils.
Shouts heard coming from the amphitheaters.
The sound of thunder if lightning didn't come first.
My father eating.
Pigs for sale in market squares squealing.

XL. Burglars

Burglars broke in and plundered Plecusa's estate, breaking the statues of Scopos.

XLI. Memories of Q. Alcimius

Quintus almost never spoke. I remember the regular, almost musical rhythm he made stirring the metal fire-pan rods before and after our lovemaking. When he spoke it was to ask for a ewer and towel to clean off his face and genitals. Or again, before evening bell striking, like a small child to ask for some ryecake.

CHAPTER III

(folio 490 verso to folio 495 recto)

XLII. Rain on the Temple of Jupiter

A fine rain falls on the gilt bronze tiles of the Capitoline Jupiter temple.

XLIII. Roman Spring

Spring dislodges us from the Janiculum slopes. 40 chariots, 110 persons, slogging along a road.

XLIV. Other Considerations on Roman Spring

In spring, colors sparkle, sounds sharpen and brighten. The villa's south wing's been fixed up. The apartments are re-done. The suite of rooms for Publius Saufeius's use this summer is readied. Add to this — that slaves, gardeners and women servants have started up on the west wing housing my own rooms. New wall-hangings will be up right after painters finish repainting. The door hinges don't squeak as they slide any more. The ceramicists have refinished the floors very competently. The overpowering smell has dredged up something from my memory — but what? A constriction narrows my throat. Not unlike a small slave of six harvests, stomach pressed to the edge of a well, struggling to pull up a chain with a bucket attached that, from darkness and cold, he can't see yet though his frail naked arms register a heaviness. Wet mortared stones echo and reecho rattlings of the chain he's tightly gripping, amplifying watery splashings that, after a kind of time-lag, fall loudly back to the water level below. What's hefted and hauled is formlessness.

XLV. Vases

The Corinthian vases.
Two Phoenician vases.

XLVI. An Unbearable Night

I couldn't stand my night. I had too much Cecuba, too much yellow turtle-dove. At the fourth watch Spurius starts snoring, gets sick to his stomach, like a drunk. Being used to it doesn't mean handling it. I kick the little slaves. I lie down in the second *exedra*. A mosquito comes by exploring my head, lights on my shoulder, then my nose, buzzing off to settle on my ear, then crawling up my cheek. If the mosquito decides to relent, squeaking chariot wheels outside will be sure to take up the slack. Again I kick the little slaves. Again I lie down next to Spurius. I get up exhausted, and unamused — not that different from Anicia Proba coming back from eating her god.

XLVII. Epigrams of C. Bassus and P. Saufeius

Tiberius Sossibianus wades into the water in a large pool.
"It's awful how he just plops his anus in," says Publius.
"I won't criticize him for plopping his anus in," says C. Bassus, "but for not keeping his mouth shut."
Publius continues —
"Tiberius Sossibianus speaks. He pollutes the air's infinity and god's dwellings. He moves his lips. The blue sky behind his face begins to get darker."

XLVIII. Auspices

One-hundred-twenty year old crows flew over the gardens twice, croaking as they passed.

XLIX. May 11, 400

Yesterday Sp. Possidius runs barefoot through the palace striking out at a bronze vase. He throws black beans seven times, and entreats the *Larvae*. *Larvae*, don't return, he cries. *Larvae*, don't return. *Larvae*, don't return. Spurius turns and falls. He's carried to his room, unconscious. Spatale looks after him.

L. Things Not to Forget

Sow vulva stuffed with mincemeat.
Two snow-cubes in Falernian wine.
Aspic from Labullan figs.

LI. Omens

Terrible omens have been ripped from the victim-entrails.

LII. Things to Do

The double arched gate overlooking the Appian Way.
The Villa at Naples and the one on the island of Megaris.

LIII. Things to Do

Being at the groves of Pompey.
Dissipations — at Marcella's.

LIV. What Lycoris Said

    Lycoris recounts this (before Publius and I knew each other). Papianilla died when Nonius Atticus Maximus was the pretorian prefect (the Nones of the month of Purifications*). P. Saufeius Minor tried to imitate the adherents of the Porch, though tears streamed down his face. He tried his usual jokes and paradoxes, but unrelenting tears furrowed his cheeks. Proceeding to the senate one day he encounters Anicia Proba. She has her servants stop the litter beside him, politely extending condolences, reminding him of her affection for him. With his lictors surrounding him, and standing straight up in his laticlave tunic,

---

* Mid-February 384.

his hands flat on his sides like a statue from the Sabine kings's era, his gaze cast down to to his red leather shoes, with his head naked and exposed to the sun, Publius wept. Anicia asked, has the time come to think on holy things, to consider what happens after death? She added, is it perhaps time to turn to the bleeding God on the cross? P. Saufeius lifted his eyes to her and said —

"How can it be time to consider holy things, the soul's afterlife, or god, when I can't even remember to wipe off the tears streaming down my face."

LV. Something to Do P. N.

I'm going to Careni.

LVI. What Q. Alcimius Said

Quintus shouted out:
"In the infinite night we can't merge our bodies."
I awoke. Beads of sweat ran down my stomach. I had been at the Rostra waiting for Silig, face to face with the Marsyas statue looming up gigantic now.

LVII. The Joys of Dawn

I love the dawn, as sun melts away shadows.
Roofs and the trees of the park as they emerge little by little.
Remembering the smells of the night, the sweat, the pleasures as, little by little, they vanish.
Little by little the body returns, concealed beneath makeup.
Cool water on my eyes, cool water in the throat.

LVIII. Litany of Sp. Possidius Barca

I order some slaves to remove an Etruscan folding bed to Spurius's bedside. I order one to carry him a *setier* of Setian wine. Morose, staring straight ahead, hands trembling, Spurius stutters:

"There was a time when I didn't exist and you didn't. Maybe there'll be a time when I don't exist though you do. Or there'll be a time when you don't exist and I do. What could be more depressing? And there'll come a time when neither of us does."

As he spoke, Spatale refilled the lamps with oil. With a finger, I stroked the back of his trembling hand.

LIX. Things Not to Forget

Mallows as laxatives.

LX. Memories of Baiae

I ate smelt and Naples pears and saw Baiae.
The south wind, odors of fruit cooked in sugar.
A red moon.

In the morning, sourrounded by servants, my great-grandmother would inspect the main garden. We weren't supposed to talk. A white misty pall lay shimmering on the seedbeds.

One day she stopped and broke silence. "Look!" she said, pointing to the grass, to something whose memory now totally escapes. I can't recall now what great-grandmother was pointing at, but looking back, I'm thinking that in the high grass, way over to the left, a nocturnal spider was still weaving its web. Dew glistened. The air was pink.

"The little frogs are back," said great-grandmother laughing loudly. "Daylight has arrived!"

CHAPTER FOUR

(folio 495 verso to folio 499 verso)

LXI. Lucianus and the Beggar Lady

Lucianus had taken in an old woman in a short yellow toga who used to beg at the north gate of the park. He had fed her. She'd asked to see me. Since Lucianus considered her talkative and entertaining, he took her to see me during *sportula*. Her toga was dirty and looked like an old yolk. It was too short and you could see her crinkly knees, her flabby thighs. I thought of an old tree-frog, her face a mass of wrinkles, a pug nose, snotty flaring nostrils. When asked her age, she answered by opening her mouth, in which there remained two rye-colored teeth. Her voice was incredibly distinguished and gentle, her language sophisticated and proud. She was 40 winters old and had just come back from Palestine. The servants approached, and we grilled her about the fate of refugees we knew. She said she wanted wine. I told a servant to bring up a *setier* of Baiae. "Do you know Quintus Alcimius?" she said, staring hard. I felt disturbed. "I suckled him through three harvests, and you offer me wine of Baiae?!" she yelled. "Tell them to bring up some Massic!" So I did as she said, ordering up some Massic. She churned out names of the dead, reams and reams of them. I took her by the arm suggesting a stroll in the park. She agreed. She had loved Quintus during the years when Flavius Afranius Syagrius was City prefect and a colleague of Antony's. She stank unmistakably. She scratched her stomach, spread her legs, and pissed loudly.

She was a bit drunk. We came to the pond. The ducks glided silently on patches of dawn. She had seated herself on the stone bench with her powerful thighs and was slapping them vigorously.

"I am Lalage Asdiga," she said. "The sea eats away at the coast to make bays. I have the mouth and backside of a sow. I was once beautiful. Time is a god of water, of crumbling cliffs, of sand. Everything empties us out and everything collapses us into death. Long ago, fruit put out on the tray lost its savor, and I was dismissed. I loved Quintus and in dreams sometimes still feel a desire for him."

Her voice was soft and her accent astonishingly pure. She got up and took me arm in arm. We went back to the palace. "I rubbed depilatories on the asses of your lovers, and you give me olives!?" she screamed as we returned within earshot of the servants. I gave orders for a basket of choice meats and sweet pastries to be made up for her. When she left, I asked Lucianus to have the little slaves run after her and give her a good whipping to keep her from even thinking about coming back.

LXII. The Dyed Woolen Stripes of P. Saufeius Minor

By the edge of a wood, I see an Egyptian blue cotton stripe approaching me. Then I see the features of Publius. Then I hear his voice: Publius praising Agorius Praetextatus.

LXIII. Things to Count On

To the list of things to count on, add the statues of the gods.

Male and female ducks, swimming in an artificial pool, drifting to the edge of a small waterfall.

An unfaithful husband casually lying to his wife, then leaving as if just having remembered something.
The cloak of goatherd.

LXIV. Things Not to Forget

We decided to stay outside the walls of Rome until October 1.*

LXV. Things Not to Forget

Sards.
Jaspers.
Buckles.
The cup attributed to Mentor.

LXVI. Things Not to Forget

A Gallic shirtwaist falling over the ass.
Teeth colored like tar.
The plundered site of Venice.

---

*The first of October, 401. Variant: "Statueramus in externis ad K. Oct. morari."

LXVII. At Marcella's

Panting in ecstasy three times at Marcella's.

LXVIII. Bags of Gold

24 bags of gold.

LXIX. Things to Do

A mongrel.
Grape-must from Laletania.

LXX. Things Said by Spatale, P. Saufeius Minor, and by Afer

Spatale had called P. Saufeius a —
"bald-headed dirty old man!"
When I first met Publius I repeated what my servant called him. Publius answered:
"I polish the top of my skull so it shines like a copper mirror, so it reflects like Apollo, like the rising sun."
He turned to the young slave, Afer, and continued:
"On the bald skull of an old man what can dust adhere to?"
Discovering an answer, Afer replied:
"The accumulated hair of the bald men of the world is crawling with lice."

LXXI. Failure of Voices

Naevia's voice suddenly becomes fragile, unsure, and inharmonious, like the voice of a someone seized with a coughing fit. What our ear hears is a kind of collapse of living voice, as at a cliff's edge. Voices like these hint at the sound of death. For a couple of seasons Spurius's voice has sounded like Naevia's. This kind of voice makes it obvious: little woolen threads hold faces in place and connect ears. The hands stay there because of these little woolen threads. And the voice hangs on a little woolen thread.

LXXII. Things Not to Forget

The fatted dormice.

LXXIII. Objects Kept from the Past

With P. Saufeius we counted up objects from the past that we'd saved. The sight of them filled us with deep emotion.

A piece of yellow colored cloth, the same yellow as you get from camomile leaves.

Two tablets belonging to Q. Alcimius on which not even three words are visible.

The two-wheeled carriage in the shed.

The spinning top of a child. Its blue — faded now, almost white.

Papianilla's hair and nails.

Publius said:

"The only object from the past is at night with the moon shining full and the ground dry, and your feet leaving no prints behind.

CHAPTER FIVE

(folio 500 recto to folio 505 verso)

LXXIV. A Memory of Q. Alcimius

On the Quirinal, Quintus knocked faintly, four times, on the shutter. I opened the door. His clothes were wet with fog. He put his arms about me. With a smile I said, take your cloak [*paenula*] off. His hair was all mussy and raindrops hung there like drops clinging to ferns. He asked for a change of linen. There was no fire-pan in the room. I took off his clothes, rubbing him dry. His toes and fingers were still ice-cold. He put his mouth to my ear and whispered a vulgarity, and suddenly I felt light-hearted, full of life.

LXXV. Things Not to Forget

The mallow laxatives.
A bath-caldron.

LXXVI. Things Not to Forget

At the baths of Titus.

LXXVII. Description of Winter

I like the bracing cold of winter, rain-free, without fog, and footsteps sounding along the lanes.
Hoarfrost on roofs and marble statues.
Hoarfrost on the done-up hair of women servants.
The unmitigated cruelty of light.
Clouds of breath exhaled by children, animals, men, little slaves hacking out ice-chunks.
I like to see charcoal burning in fire-pans, bodies turning to them. Different parts of the body moving into them, from desire or whim.

LXXVIII. Catarrhs

Awful catarrhs. My left forehead throbbing in pain. A cough keeps me awake. Publius Saufeius comes to see me. I can't get my breath.
"There's a trace of ash in your heart," he says. "What we've been through, together — it's not utterly consumed. A trace of ash in your heart impedes your breathing."

LXXIX. What P. Saufeius Minor Said

P. Saufeius's head was wrapped in a blue woolen bandage. He had a yellow hood over it. I coughed. Spatale brought in herbal tea, the mulled wine. Marulla poured oil into lamps. The sky was inky, like an octopus all of a sudden shooting black. I couldn't stop coughing. Publius coughed himself. I remembered Spurius. I spoke of dying.

"There's no need to be frightened," Publius told me. "I'll be the first to be straw-man.* It's all of our fate. To get tossed into the arena of the dead."

LXXX. Things Not to Forget

In April she'll cross the Tiber at Porto.

LXXXI. Things to Remember

Soles of old shoes falling apart in the mud.

LXXXII. Signs of Happiness

Signs of happiness — inherited wealth.
Precision in language, an accent that consists in not having an accent.
A park with variety and shade and rolling hills.
Physical robustness.
A variety of friends, loquacious, knowing how to read. But also the indulgent guest who on occasion can slip easily into vulgarity.

---

*A pun on "prima pila." Referring to the first dummy thrown to bulls in the ring, to goad them on. Consequently, torn to pieces. Metaphorically "prima pila" means a rag, a dust rag

The face of a man whose eyes reflect a whole range of emotion like mirrors from Levant.
Sleeping five hours as long as it's uninterruped.
The company of a man fond of pleasure — meaning pleasure as a type of good manners.
A moderate fear, in response to death.
Taking a bath.
Using the lyre.

LXXXIII. Something Sp. Possidius Barca Used to Say

Spurius said — and was this 10 or 13 harvests ago — he could stick Publius's ass inside Marius's and would anything be left?

LXXXIV. Happiness

Happiness. Wandering the Saburnian road.
The eleventh hour. Gossip. Merchants closing up.
Receiving the Vitellian tablets.
Drunkenness before sleep.

LXXXV. Things Not to Forget

Pennyroyal against coughing.
The mallow emollients.
Sassina cheeses.

LXXXVI. Epigram of P. Saufeius Minor

Publius formulated this epigram on M. Pollio's cowardly behavior —
"On all fours, he laps up the dog's water."

LXXXVII. What Nasica Smells Like

Nasica comes to see me. On the advice of Melania, Nasica turned Christian, was anointed by the sacrificer, and was given the name Paulina. I tell her suddenly:
"You smell quite strongly. Consult Sotodes."
Paulina maintains that a virgin's body can be given to the curious and sometimes immodest motions of cleansing at most once a week. "This body of filth," says Paulina. Laughingly, I say, one look at you convinces me of that! I don't ask for details about a whim she has, ill-befitting a body reserved for gods, untouched, shedding layers of filth. When Paulina sits down, why does she dust off the seat she's about to sit on? She should dust off her own rear-end before sitting.

LXXXVIII. Things Not to Forget

Pennyroyal for coughs
Sassina cheese.

LXXXIX. Sickness of Sp. Possidius Barca

I had the slaves take a folding bed and open it beside Spurius. He was drooling. I bent over. He smelled like decay, like a chick hatching out of an egg. I sat on the edge of the folding bed and rested my hand on my husband's chest. I told him, you stink like a dead dog. He said — "to remind you of little Muola's furry odor." He added — "you don't have to put yourself to the trouble of visiting me like this or at least you don't need to stay so long at the end of the day. " I said:

"I'll stop coming the day you smell like the farts of an Egyptian hippopotamus."

Spurius had the good grace to laugh. Later, I took from Mommeius's hands the large basin he intended to put under his master's mouth. Assisted by Spatale, helping him sit up, I stuck my finger into his mouth to make him vomit. At the first watch he dozed. I stayed near and told the slave to go get Sotodes. I consulted him. I had him show me the urine and feces of the day. Cladus prepared a horosccope.

At nightfall, after the oil lamps were filled and put up on the walls, after Spatale, Flaviana, Marulla and myself had washed Spurius's body using a sponge soaked in solution of myrrh, milk and foliat, stammering and prompted by a sudden whim, Spurius asks to have his clients, servants and slaves withdraw. Even Flaviana has to go. He settles down. He speaks to me for some time, although he becomes more and more incoherent, babbling, like a child. I bend over not so much to hear what he's saying, but to listen to the drone of that voice in which gentleness and the weakness of death had imperceptibly joined sleep's stupor.

Spurius spoke of journeys we'd planned for the summer. I slipped my fingers into his hands. It's hard for me to recognize my husband — in the large, aged, naked, pink, depilated, wrinkled body, glistening with sweat. I see an awkward body rolled in fetal position, sucking up fear like mother's milk and drowsing off. For a moment I study him, as he sleeps soundly. What's so surprising is, with left hand already consigned to Rhadamantes, and right to Eachus, the crown of the skull caught in Charu's net, denying the obvious — he'd think of his sickness as only temporary, not feel the death already touching him. At dinner I had murene filets, sow-nipple points, grilled clams, sugar beets, and two *setiers* of dark thick wine of Opimius.

XC. Sickness of Sp. Possidius Barca

A man who, during life, worries about his health, his porcelain teeth, his oncoming old age and death in deaths of freinds. This man refuses to see his own death. He suddenly expects remission. He multiplies plans made ridiculous by the state of his body. He dins this into the ears of a woman who knows its hopelessness.

A man who confuses what's actually a viper's body — with the reflection of the bow he carries.

XCI. Things to Do

Cinnamon and balm.

XCII. Death of Sp. Possidius Barca

He stammers out the name Gabba, then says a few things lacking coherence. As Leitus and Philo apply poultices to the legs and as, with Spatale's help, Flaviana makes final preparations for the pennyroyal in the goblet, he turns his face to me, searching with his eyes, gently raising those eyebrows, smiling a bit, his face more distant, more unhappy. I put my hand into his. We all go about our business silently. Marulla pours oil in the lamps. A little gurgling noise catches in Spurius's throat. As if caught by a mute contagion, one after another, we come to a complete halt. Then we weep and wail.

XCIII. Things That Smell Good

Myrtle.
A red saffron from Corycos.
The aroma of blossoming vine.
Ground-up amber.
Nard and myrrh to make foliat.

XCIV. Things Not to Forget

Juice from the Chelidonian isles.
8 balls of aphronite.

XCV. Things to Do

Interest due on the Kalends.

XCVI. Bags of Gold

24 bags of gold.

XCVII. A Thing Said by Sp. Possidius Barca

After Spurius died, nothing particular came to mind. This morning I thought of something he said on his deathbed, that moved me:
"There's not another life. We won't see each other again."
Our tears fell. We held hands.

CHAPTER SIX

(folio 506 recto to folio 512 recto)

XCVIII. *Children's Games*

    Little children playing with stones, gleaming reddish brown, like their tiny hands.

XCIX *Children's Games*

    At Veii near Matrinia when we were ten years old, at midday with the sun directly above, we found Manius and Decimus in the stable. They were asleep on piles of straw in the shade of a shed out in back. We crept close trying to stifle hysterical giggling. Darkness, the strong smell of the animals, straw, cow dung, and urine quickened our pulses. You could make out huge haywagon wheels, alternating bands of sunshine and shadow playing on wooden latticework. Moisture still glistened on the plowshare blades, resting against the wall. Cotton-mouthed, we crept up on Manius's fat calves and sprung. Amid midday reflections of plowshares, sweaty gleaming skins, awkward glances, gold grain, and golden dust afloat in the light, cackling chickens, whoops and outbursts of laughter, we saw Decimus's and Manius's bodies discharging. Neither was old enough to have a haircut. Manius's little tunic was torn. That evening we were punished. I remember that, getting up, my hand brushed Decimus's thigh. I felt the fresh liquid of its sticky consistency. I blushed. I looked at Decimus. Beet-red, he returned the glance.

C. *Caristia Gifts*

Caristia.
6 children of my daughter Flaviana and tiny Lucius.
7 little ones, from my daughter Vetustina.
2 children of my son Cnaeus.
12 of my son Fabricius.
4 of my son Sextus.
8 children and 2 grandchildren of my daughter Aufidia.
3 little ones of my daughter Plecusa.*

CI. *Plecusa Plays with her Rings*

My daughter Plecusa aggravates me, playing continuously with the rings I gave her on Caristia.

---

*Februrary 22, 406. Caristia was a strictly family celebration in the course of which family members exchanged gifts.

CII. Things to Remember

Naples pears.
Wrinkled grapes.
Tripe — from the Falisci region.
Children's guppies.

CIII. Bags of Gold

24 bags of gold.

CIV. Something Said by P. Saufeius Minor

Publius turned to Ti. Sossibianus saying:
"From the time the world has been a living being, the house has been on fire. The fact that the world is on fire makes the world so bright."

CV. Something Said by Plecusa

Plecusa said of her husband — his ass is as hairy as his soul is smooth.

CVI. Things to Do

Interest due on the Kalends.

CVII. Bassus Suggests a Hypothesis on the Origin of Odors

Caius begins to speak about odors, making a hypothesis about the origins of unpleasant smells:

"Before our birth we are cadavers from a life we don't recall and we float at the bottom of the ocean.

"During the time our mothers bear us, we become swollen, puffed up with air. We rot. Little by little we rise to the surface of that ocean.

"Unexpectedly birth tosses us on the shore. Like a sort of sudden violent wave. T. Lucretius Carus said: on each day of life we touch shores of light.

"As the sun's rays hit us, we start to feel [get rancid and stink]. And we start shouting.

"At death we rejoin the depths, the silence, the odorless sweetness of the abyss."

CVIII. What Lycoris Said

Charinus loves the young before they get beards. Charinus desires Lycoris's sons. Lycoris says when he eyes Servius and Aulus, his lips pucker.

CIX. Things Not to Forget

4 pieces of Batavian soap.
200 linen filters for the jars.
200 dessert spoons.
Babylonian tapestries.

CX. Recommendations to her Daughter Flavinia

I took Flaviana aside and said:

I don't advise rimming Nicomachus. As he'll get used to these attentions, when the day comes and you're bored or you have a migraine or your back is out, you won't be up to it. Besides, he'll lose interest in a more appropriate place, one that makes fewer demands on you. Keep in mind the long haul, not a pitch of delight that's not sustainable. To gently and regularly control a man's pleasures is to rule his head by ruling his moods. To rule his head and his moods is to rule his wealth, property, servants, palace and glory, if not dreams and thoughts. To rule his moods, his palaces, and his glory is better than to rule his dreams and thoughts.

CXI. Things to Do

Interest on the Kalends.

CXII. On Babies

I don't like being around babies, trying to placate their petulant screams, wiping their noses, drying their tears because a nurse of theirs has been punished with a whipping, or has left, or is dead, and at the same time playing with them for hours on end.

CXIII. Something Not to Forget

Grattius's vase.

CXIV. Things Not to Forget

A lizard-fish.
Eggs cooked in ashes.
A minutal.
A cheese bread baked in the Velabre area.
A cheap Vatican table wine worse than a Spoleto.

CXV. Tarentos Makes the Children Laugh

Tarentos sings "Remus reports to the office of the Pretorian Guard." He swings his head and torso. He's very funny. When he gets his breath, his cock hangs out, his belly pushes up his tunic. The children giggle and Lucius and his cousin Aulus make a game of imitating him.

CXVI. Pedantry of P. Saufeius on the Young Slave of Plecusa

Plecusa's young slave is very handsome. Publius cites two verses from Philomusus Zetes:
Beauty disappearing with the sound of his voice.
A galley such as sea might swallow.

CXVII. A Saying of P. Saufeius on the Kitchens

P. Saufeius says, a village works in my kitchens. Sometimes I visit the ovens. I divert myself with spatulas and wood-veined spoons. I get hold of the knives and I cut.

CXVIII. Bags of Gold

24 bags of gold.

CXIX. Good Advice from P. Saufeius

Publius passes by the door. I say to him:
"First I'm alone. Second I'm old. Third I'm afraid."
"That has no shadow. Being alone, old, or fearful doesn't cast a shadow on the ground. Repeat: this casts no shadow. Nothing of what you interpret about the world has a shadow in the world."
Publius gently sits down. He arranges the woolen head-band about his neck and naked skull. Publius says with an effort:
"Feelings don't exist. Words invent useless existences. We mustn't use any other words than those referring to objects leaving a shadow on this earth, in the light proper to this earth."

CXX. Eye Ailments

I have a runny eye. My left eye's as hard as a green olive still on the branch. The eyeball hardens and protrudes, sometimes pus exudes from it. I can barely manage in the cold of dawn to scratch this on wood tablets. Publius says:
"A kind of invisible dust falls from the sun, full of atoms, a dust that nothing can wipe away, a dust that swells in the eye, a dust that utterly thickens in death's night."
Publius continues:
"This dust is called dust."
He remains silent, then continues:
"Or else the name of this dust is time."
Again he's silent, again continues:
"Or else the name of this dust is earth."

Again he's silent, and continues:
"Or else the name of this dust of dusts is still dust."
"The god Orcus?"
"I'm sure there's a meaning dustier than dust, and I'm sure there's a meaning dustier than the god Orcus."
We drank.

CXXI. Confidences of Sp. Saufeius Minor

Publius arrives with his cane, with Gallic cloak, swathed in an Egyptian woolen headband. Publius is my oldest friend. All of a sudden he confesses to me that the death of Spurius moved him to happiness. He confides:

"I loved Papianilla very much. In days gone by I — truly and greatly — loved Papianilla. There's also the fact that I found a beauty in lettuce leaves, in their color, in their freshness, in the forms they display, and still more in the desires they quench. And there's also the fact I appreciated books redolent of old laurel. I very much liked rubbing my beard with scrolls. Now I understand. Wine doesn't quiet desire in me, but, in a way that each day I find more permissive and helpful, it takes on the job of not awakening memories in me.

"My little reader no longer strokes my *mentula*. He opens the great codices and in dawn hours or at twilight I doze peacefully or relax without catching much of what's read to me, though I listen to the sound of my tongue repeating it and this moves me.

"For a long time I've felt desire for Apronenia and didn't dare tell her."

CXXII. Bags of Gold

24 bags of gold.

CXXIII. Properties of Air

In the palace of P. Saufeius Minor, the subject under consideration is air.

"Air serves to carry off souls of men who are dead," says Caius Bassus.

"In expiring, the dead suddenly give back their brief loan of breath," says Flaviana.

"Air serves to stir the flowers of the pear-tree we see over there at the left, in the sunbeam falling on the mulberry tree," says Herulicus.

"To allow us to speak like fools," says Lycoris.

"To exhale," says Ti. Sossibianus heaving a great sigh.

"To give us the possibility of laboring with our breath, of choking, and of dying," says Publius.

CXXIV. Thing to Remember

Pumice stone for papyrus.

CXXV. A Woman Wiping up Little Puddles of Spilled Time

A woman loving the sound of wood. A woman with a tablet. A woman playing on wax. A woman sharpening the edge of her stylus. A woman concealing a too large, too loose vagina. A woman making use of an old piece of cloth. A woman wiping up little puddles of spilled time.

CXXVI. Plans of P. Saufeius Minor

These are some plans occuring to Publius in the banquet hall of his palace:

To keep warm with the help of the products of woods, and of the seasons.

To land a fish quivering at the end of the line, and reel it in with a single finger.

On a rough table, to put out light honey in a pot of red clay.

In cinders on a hearth, to listen to a hen's egg cooking.

We laughed. We laughed till tears flowed.

CXXVII. Melancholy Evening

A heavenly vault, distant and black. I was tired, had an upset stomach, tried to vomit. An impulse told me to throw myself off the edge of a cliff. On top of this there was an intense impulse to throw myself off the earth to heaven's void. I had a servant haul up mulled Syrian wine, which made me spit up bile. I stayed alone near the fire-pan. Spatale came in, to light the lamps. She came to me, put my head on her belly. I asked her to leave. I fell suddenly to my knees. From the fire-pan I grabbed a piece of deadened charcoal and on a marble pavement I scribbled the letter Q. So doing, I collapsed sobbing.

CHAPTER SEVEN

(folio 512 to folio 518 recto)

CXXVIII. Small Sparrows

In the hedge and on a bare tree and dry, stone wall, small sparrows feed their young.
I thought — a palace in ruins.
A dance of servants, wet-nurses, babies, feeding on a finger.

CXXIX. Things Not to Forget

Flaviana yesterday at Coru.
Today at Terracina.
Tomorrow at Formiae.

CXXX. Things Not to Forget

Interest due at the Kalends.
Sandals.

CXXXI. Things Not to Forget

Think about polishing toenails.

CXXXII. Things That Last and Things That Don't

To the list of things that last, I'll add childhood.
Arborescent shrubs.
When waiting for Aulus, who's at the grammarian's, and should have been back more than an hour before this.
Old age.
A sea tortoise.
The death of the dead.
Insomnia.
Crows.
Among things that don't last, you overlooked the immortal gods and impeccable craftsmanship.
Among things that don't last, subtract love. It belongs to our species like sex organs or the accompanying breasts making possible reproduction but not defining anything particularly human.

CXXXIII. Exciting Sounds

To the list of exciting sounds, you'll add a lover's voice heard from behind a hedge, from inside litter curtains, from behind a door, or a brocade tapestry.
The Setia accent. This was Latronia's. She was from Setia. She was quite young and cheerful and quite lovely. She was murdered the year of Magnence's death. D. Avitius forbade me to go near the body.

When I hear exciting sounds from a dice cup, my face flushes brightly, my heart's like a wine skin dipped in a stream by the goatherds, then greedily lifted up to lips.

CXXXIV. *A Monk Come from the East*

Amnia, a monk from the East with a handsome face from the Indus valley, clothed like a king and surrounded with numerous clientele, presented himself at the gate of P. Saufeius's palace located on Mount Caelius. Fronto* had him come in, going to the second *tablinum,* asking him to sit and await his master. Thereupon Fronto informed Publius — who, in the company of Caius Bassus and Tiberius Sossibianus, was listening to Calpetanus and Olus compete with the lyre. Publius rises to his feet and, suddenly ablaze with anger, spits at the floor, ripping off the blue woolen headband tightly wound on his forehead. He issues orders. Amnia's to be thrown out of the palace precints, if necessary using rocks. Caius asked him — why this reaction? Aren't you breaking the laws of hospitality? Rearranging the blue woolen headband on his forehead Publius says:

"The idea that the world's a dream is itself a dream."

CXXXV. *Another Observation of P. Saufeius Minor On the Gods*

Having had a bit to drink Publius has this to say about the gods and humans in the universe:

---

*P. Saufeius Minor's steward, responsible for Saufeius's palace on Mount Caelius.

"The absence of the gods adds to the splendor of the universe. Humans** diminish the splendor of the universe [or else: Humans diminish the universe by lending it splendor]."

CXXXVI. Confidences of P. Saufeius Minor

Publius says he can never sleep. He rises. He wanders naked and drowsy, yawning. He opens a set of doors. Sometimes he sits, dreaming of sleep. He smiles. He's dreaming of at last losing consciousness.

CXXXVII. An Observation of P. Saufeius Minor

P. Saufeius looked at Aufida's and Flaviana's children, running through the park bedecked in its spring colors, with the gardeners at work. Publius observes:
"Children have the grace of small squirrels."

CXXXVIII. Things Not to Forget

Interest due on the Kalends.
36 bags of gold.
Crystal cups cut in embroidery pattern.
8 cyathuses.
A sedan chair.

** "Homines" not "viri"

CXXXIX. Spatale's Teeth

Spatale puts a plum in her mouth. It must be sour. Opening her mouth and grimacing, she shows she has no teeth.

CXL. Something Not to Forget

Laurentian boar.

CXLI. Something Not to Forget

Drinking Sabine wine. Never again.

CXLII. Observation of P. Saufeius Minor

Publius said there exists neither suffering nor content nor disappointment nor hope.
"In the name of what do you make complaints or feel suffering? What assumptions are made about the universe in feeling unhappy? What assumptions are made when you assume that you hold happiness in your hands or in a body that substantiates that hope? Birth, sunlight, bodily shape, civil society, air, death, have they no significance?"

CXLIII. *Observation of Ti. Sossibianus*

Tiberius Sossibianus holds his love-handles and says: "After each sweet thought, I give Afer a good stuffing!"

CXLIV. *Human Fate*

In company with his little slave, Afer, and in company with P. Saufeius, M. Pollio, and C. Bassus, Ti. Sossibianus speaks of the fate of the Empire and of gains made by the religious parties. M. Pollio turns to Publius asking — what's in the future? What's to be man's fate in days to come?

"First, all bodily functions that link us with other animals. Next, two or three kinds of behavior that set us off from those animals. I refer to putting on clothes, taking them off, engaging in conversation. Finally, spending time doing this, that, and the other thing, and ending up breathing your last. That's the fate of humans living in ages to come."

CXLV. *Something Not to Forget*

Interest on the Kalends.

CXLVI. *P. Saufeius Minor and Licinius Sura*

Publius is wrapped in his woolen headband, his knees are thin, his calves non-existent, his hands always in motion, his deep voice uttering the language of the ancient Romans — with the care and purity of a book by Licinius Sura. You think it's a man moving you, and you're hearing a book by Licinius Sura.

CXLVII. A Date at the Rostra

The day I'm scheduled to see Quintus and Silig at the forum, near the Rostra by the Marsyas statue. Silig's late. Quintus suddenly spits at the ground and says:

"You need, number one, a depilatory, number two, two porcelain teeth, number three, some pounded Venice clay, and number four, your youth."

"Will you please leave?" I said. "Will you just go?"

Priam's wife couldn't have been more prim or starched. I remained insensible for several hours — during which, strictly speaking, I saw the Gorgon. For several hours I saw the Gorgon, then broke down sobbing.

CXLVIII. Things Not to Forget

On the porch of Europe.
Ludi Megalenses.
Ludi Cereales.

CXLIX. Dream

At the end of the night I had this dream:

I'm holding Pompey's head made of lard. It's quite hot outside and I'm in a field running anxiously. On no account can I allow Pompey's head to melt. I look in vain for a hut or the shade of a tree. I see a huge oak, dense with foliage. I rush to it.

At its feet (looking unsuccessfully) there's no trace of shade. What I still remember of the dream blurs here. Below me I see Publius Saufeius under the arch of a viaduct, although his body is naked. It's the body of a robust and oiled gymnast. His abdomen is depilated. His cock, if not erect, at least is quite thick and red. I hold out my hands toward the gymnast's body. With pebbles splaying out from beneath me, I run through the gorge and reach bottom. I go round a massive pillar holding up the viaduct, but the nearer I get to Publius, the more his body turns from me. He turns his back, and his buttocks grow, till seeming gigantic. A rushing torrent separates me from the athlete's ass. I look at my hands. They're empty and covered with fat. I'm hysterical since I obviously let go of Pompey's head while running. I search the bushes and mosses covering the torrent's rocks. I lift up the black, humid stones and discover only fat white worms and then — my mother's quite irate face. Anxiety increases. With difficulty I lift the last rock, which is heavier and circular. My fingers slip. I arch my back, manage to lift it. Under the rock is a scrawny little elm, under the leaves of which is P. Saufeius. The elm tree itself is pathetic but its shade is deep, magnificent, and very cool. Cautiously and respectfully P. Saufeius emerges from the tree's shade. He seems tired, has deep circles under his eyes, deeply etched wrinkles. He strides slowly through the immense shadow of the little elm, and a sort of whitish liquid exudes along his thigh. He turns to the shade of the tree, addressing to it an incomprehensible speech, pronouncing the words in exaggerated fashion. He turns to me, face shining, looking straight at me, then slowly approaches to touch me. At the very moment his nose is about to touch mine, I see all at once it's not Publius Saufeius, and I'm confused by this. With growing anxiety, I can't seem to recognize the features of the face — but I know that I know him. Then the man quickly retreats. The elm, the stranger, the circle of shade, the sun, the whole scene suddenly is quite far away, no bigger than my finger. The tiny man leans forward ceremoniously, thanking the tree for the shade provided him.

CHAPTER EIGHT

(folio 518 verso to folio 524 recto)

CL. Calpetanus Tunes his Lyre and Sings

The servants place folding chairs around the fire-pan. Darkness fills the sky. The water for tisane and honey is boiled, with a hint of hot mulled wine to it. Calpetanus enters with us and tunes his lyre. He strikes up the Salian song and the song of the Arvali brothers. In the silence, we consider the outline of our toenails.

CLI. Things Not to Forget

At the Saepta a pedestal table in lemon wood.
A hydraulic organ.
Two embroidered togas.
Four feet of ivory at 800,000 sesterces.

CLII. Bags of Gold

24 bags of gold.

CLIII. Things Not to Forget

Tablets.
Green-veined Laconian marble.

CLIV. Sadness in Spatale

Spatale heats up a cup of Falernian wine, weeps and sniffles. She can't bring herself to pronounce the name Marcus.

CLV. Signs of Old Age

Spatale has stopped depilating her vulva.

CLVI. Orifices of the Body

It seems to me that my body's nine orifices gape open meaninglessly. Have they started realizing they're opening up on a void? My nine orifices start conversing with death's silence.

CLVII. Plan to Leave for Sicily

I make a suggestion to Publius. Come with me to Sicily, to the villa Spurius repurchased from Anicia Proba. With the devastations on our minds, we looked out at the evening from the terrace attached to the Albina grove, beyond the narrows, as smoke from conflagrations mingled with the evening's fog.

Publius shrugs. Gently he asks:

"Devastations? What devastations?"

CLVIII. Things Doing Away with Boredom

To the number of things doing away with boredom, I'll add wine.

Malicious evil, spoken about friends and family.

The game of backgammon.

Fruit.

Washing.

Considering the image of yourself as reflected in black Bithynian marble.

Dreams of gifts from questors.

Unrolling a book.

Taking up the lyre.

Going down to the kitchens and eating.

CLIX. Things that Melt the Heart

On a list of things that melt the heart, you didn't mention an enthusiastic youngster, full of love of life, singing away, full-tilt.

The indispositions of the old.

A child who kills his pet thrush or puppy from curiosity, his hands still bloody. He tortures the cat with gloved hands. With his little copper sword he torments a red and white weasel.

Quite young people nose to nose, whom modesty makes awkward, or whom our presence suddenly interrupts, holding them in embarrassed silence.

The sight of a piece of floating blue scarf, glimpsed from a litter — at the far end of a lane.

Quite old persons quarreling.

The man you love breaking suddenly into tears without having had anything to drink, for no apparent reason. Less tears in this case, than a trembling lip.

CLX. Observations of Lycoris

With Lycoris I spoke of my plan to leave for Sicily. Lycoris was of Publius's opinion.

"The nest of the wild swan is a floating raft," says Lycoris wryly.

"Likewise the moorhen's nest," riposts Publius naughtily.

"Likewise too the crested grebe's nest," contributes Lycoris.

We drank resinous wine. We ate filets or moray eel and African pomegranates.

CLXI. Bags of Gold A. D. XVII Kal.

6 times 5 bags of gold A. D. XVII Kal.

CLXII. Things to Do

A little honey from Hybla mixed with a little honey from Hymettus.

CLXIII. At P. Saufeius Minor's Bedside

I went to Mount Caelius. I passed through the palace, black with its ant-like visitors. I went to P. Saufeius's large reception room and sat down at his bedside. His Egyptian woolen headband was unwrapped and his skull was naked. He was hugging a saffron-hued *endromis* to his body. On a little marble table were placed some extremely licentious books, among which I recognized Sybaris and Mussetius. I remembered the old days — gossip whispered in our ears, the recollection of Julian's victories. The room smelled of an old fuller's earth jar suddenly breaking open on a street. My only thought was to go back to the two-wheeled carriage, return to the slopes of Janiculum, where cool winds play among the leaves on trees and part the hair of the men in the park.

Publius shivered. He had the body of a boy of 10 winters, his skin translucent. Bored, you could have counted his bones. At first, the power of his emotions prevented speech. He gazed at me. He seemed a man held in thrall to some great dread, or again — a mercenary in battle as the god Pan swoops, sowing alarm and confusion. He made light of the situation. He needed to appear brave. He flirted. He likened himself to ancient statues, bit by bit disintegrated by a very small fig tree. His voice lacked clarity and depth. At last he felt up to social chit-chat, some small talk. He recalled dead friends, our age, his illness. He fretted over sleeplessness. He complained about the cold he felt. He pouted like a child about the fever that would carry him away. He had servants bring in Opimius wine in snow, which I found excellent.

I tried to calm him down. He panted, saliva trickling down his breasts. Evening came. I imagined the dark, moist cave, mosses spreading on the Diaulus fresco.

Two old friends whose bodies are unable to recognize each other. Two old bags of excrement and words, made from skins mottled with spots of Erebus, gossiping like Egeria and Numa in the darkness of a cave.

CLXIV. Things to Do

At the Saepta, tears of Heliades.
The temple of Serapis.
Two alabaster flasks from Cosmus.

CLXV. Omen

I visited Publius. M. Pollio and Ti. Sossibianus, accompanied by young Afer, were on the point of leaving. It was snowing outside. I kissed Afer. Publius didn't open his eyes. He panted in sleep, upper lip beaded in sweat. Motionless, listening to my friend's breath, in my ear I heard the words and cadences of a song. I recalled the song *The Sound of the Cranes Echoing Along the Strymon*. I remembered the very lovely young Latronia singing that song. I remembered her cheeks blushing. Again, I saw her two great eyes sparkling.

CLXVI. Something P. Saufeius Said about Death

Marcus Pollio tells this story — something Publius said. Publius, Marcus, Herulicus, Tiberius, and Afer were speaking about the gods of ancient Romans, the gods of the Greek philosophers, and the soul's immortality. Publius suddenly said: "I saw God in my childhood. He had my mother's features. I swear, after that, the thought of afterlife ceases to be attractive."

CLXVII. Things to Do

Interest on the Kalends.

CLXVIII. Things to Do

Interest on the Kalends.

CLXIX. Death of P. Saufeius Minor

Spatale enters the room, tears her tunic, tells me P. Saufeius died that evening. The news doesn't affect me. Speaking of our youth, Publius had compared it to an old amphora without label. I pictured an old amphora. Then I pictured a headband of Egyptian wool around the opening of the old amphora. I shared this image with Spatale. The latter looked at me, frowning. She scolded as if I'd said something disrespectful.

CLXX. Things to Do

Two cockfights this evening.

CLXXI. Things to Do

Three cockfights this evening.

CLXXII. Things to Do

Four cockfights this evening.

CLXXIII. Bags of Gold

24 bags of gold.

CLXXIV. A Memory of P. Saufeius Minor

Publius explained everything by tracing it to Tullus Hostilius's era.

CLXXV. Something Not to Forget

A Setia fig.

CLXXVI. Things Not to Forget

Bream and magpie.

CLXXVII. A Vandal Nurse Belonging to the Hasding Clan

Pecusa's old nurse, originally a Vandal, explained to us she's a member of the Hasding clan. During the night I dream this:
A baby begging for milk, playing with the brownish tip of the nipple, sends out piercing cries and pounds its woe-begone mother's breasts.

CLXXVIII. Mount Caelius

Verdigris erodes Hector's helmet. Several millennia. It turns into a tiny sprig of green grass, beneath Trojan walls.

CLXXIX. Something Not to Forget

A little Setia wine in a crystal goblet at noon.

CLXXX. A Memory of Sp. Possidius Barca

At the banquet at Marcella's, an absolutely drunk Spurius blubbering and stammering:
"We're not animals."
We laugh till we cry.

CLXXXI. A Walk on Mount Viminal

Publius loved the hill's willow trees.

CLXXXII. Walking through the Park on Mount Janiculum

Strolling through the park on Mount Janiculum when unexpectedly a child of three winters slips its fingers into yours, mottled with flowers from the field of the dead. Then the heart skips its beat. Then your cheeks, summarily attached to this wicker skeleton, turn hectic red. (Or else: a memory of a color turns the memory of the cheeks crimson). Accomplished students of happiness and experts in the full range of pleasure and joy — what leads us now to acknowledge another kind of learning in us, an understanding to which there remain deep inside us an indefinite number of witnesses?

CLXXXIII. Young Girls by Lamplight

Young girls crowded together in a corner of the atrium, their faces young, fresh, candid, happy, timid, and open. They're all turned toward the lamp, looking out to shadows beyond, laughing. The lamplight pours from all those eyes, reflects on all those cheeks, and covers those delicate, girlish, and outstretched fingers with little layers of gold.

NOTE

Pascal Quignard was born in 1948 in Verneuil. In 1994 he resigned from his jobs (Secretary General of Editions Gallimard and President of the International Festival of Baroque Opera and Theater at Versailles) in order to devote himself entirely to writing.

He has published eighty-four *Little Treatises*, many novels, translations from the Latin (Albucius, Porcius Latro), the Chinese (Kong-souen Long), and the Greek (Lycophron). Among his many honors is the coveted "Prix des Critiques."

The film, *All the World's Mornings* (directed by Alain Corneau), was made from Quignard's novel of the same title (Graywolf Press). Two other novels were published in English: *Albucius* (The Lapis Press) and *The Salon in Württemberg* (Grove Weidenfeld). Burning Deck has published his poem, *Sarx*.

Among his other titles are:
L'être du balbutiement: Essai sur Sacher-Masoch, MdF, 1969
La parole de la Délie: Essai sur Maurice Scève, MdF, 1974
Le lecteur, Gallimard, 1976
Sang, Orange Export Ltd., 1976
Hiems, Orange Export Ltd., 1977
Carus, Maeght Editeur, 1979
Sur le défaut de terre, Clivages, 1979
La leçon de musique, Hachette, 1987
Les escaliers de Chambord, Gallimard, 1989
Petits Traités I-VIII, Maeght Editeur, 1990
Le nom sur le bout de la langue, P.O.L., 1993

Bruce X has, under the name Bruce Boone, written fiction (*Century of Clouds, My Walk with Bob*) and essays on Duncan, Spicer, O'Hara. Beside Quignard's novel *Albucius*, he has translated *Guilty* and *On Nietzsche* by George Bataille, and *Pacific Wall* by Jean-François Lyotard. He lives in San Francisco.

SERIE d'ECRITURE

No. 1: Alain Veinstein, *Archeology of the Mother* (tr. Tod Kabza, Rosmarie Waldrop), 1986

No. .2: Emmanuel Hocquard, *Late Additions* (tr. Connell McGrath, Rosmarie Waldrop), 1988

No. 3: Anne-Marie Albiach, Marcel Cohen, Jean Daive, Dominique Fourcade, Jean Frémon, Paol Keineg, Jacqueline Risset, Jacques Roubaud, Claude Royet-Journoud (tr. Anthony Barnett, Charles Bernstein, Lydia Davis, Serge Gavronsky, Rachel Stella, Keith Waldrop, Rosmarie Waldrop), 1989

No. 4: Anne-Marie Albiach, Olivier Cadiot, Danielle Collobert, Edith Dahan, Serge Fauchereau, Dominique Fourcade, Liliane Giraudon, Joseph Guglielmi, Vera Linhartova, Anne Portugal (tr. Charles Bernstein, Norma Cole, Robert Kocik, Natasha, Ron Padgett, Keith Waldrop, Rosmarie Waldrop), 1990

No. 5: Joseph Guglielmi, *Dawn* (tr. Rosmarie Waldrop), 1991

No. 6: Jean Daive, *A Lesson in Music* (tr. Julie Kalendek), 1992

No. 7: Pierre Alferi, Jean-Pierre Boyer, Olivier Cadiot, Dominique Fourcade, Jean Frémon, Jean-Marie Gleize, Dominique Grandmont, Emmanuel Hocquard, Isabelle Hovald, Anne Portugal, Jacques Roubaud, James Sacré, Anne Talvaz, Esther Tellerman (tr. David Ball, Norma Cole, Stacy Doris, Paul Green, Tom Mandel, Pam Rehm, Cole Swensen, Keith Waldrop, Rosmarie Waldrop), 1993

No. 8: Paol Keineg, *Boudica* (tr. Keith Waldrop), 1994

No. 9: Marcel Cohen, *The Peacock Emperor Moth* (tr. Cid Corman), 1995

No. 10: Jacqueline Risset, *The Translation Begins* (tr. Jennifer Moxley), 1996

No. 11: Alain Veinstein, *Even a Child* (tr. Robert Kocik, Rosmarie Waldrop), 1997

No. 12: Emmanuel Hocquard, *A Test of Solitude* (tr. Rosmarie Waldrop), 2000

No. 13/14: *Crosscut Universe: Writing on Writing from France* (ed./tr. Norma Cole) 2000

No. 15: Pascal Quignard, *On Wooden Tablets: Apronenia Avitia* (tr. Bruce X), 2001

No. 16: Esther Tellerman, *Extreme War* (tr. Keith Waldrop), 2002

SERIE d'ECRITURE SUPPLEMENTS:

No. 1: Claude Royet-Journoud, *i.e.* (tr. Keith Waldrop), 1995

No. 2: Pascal Quignard, *Sarx* (tr. Keith Waldrop), 1997

No. 3: Anne-Marie Albiach, *A Geometry* (tr. Keith Waldrop, Rosmarie Waldrop), 1998